W9-ACE-601

SAN DIEGO   AUSTIN   ORLANDO

GULLIVER
BOOKS
HARCOURT
BRACE
JOVANOVICH

THE CHINESE MIRROR

ADAPTED FROM
A KOREAN FOLKTALE BY

MIRRA GINSBURG

ILLUSTRATED BY

MARGOT ZEMACH

WESTPORT PUBLIC LIBRARY
WESTPORT, CONNECTICUT

J
348.2
Gi

Text copyright © 1988 by Mirra Ginsburg
Illustrations copyright © 1988 by Margot Zemach

All rights reserved. No part of this publication
may be reproduced or transmitted in any form or
by any means, electronic or mechanical, including
photocopy, recording, or any information storage
and retrieval system, without permission in
writing from the publisher.

Requests for permission to make copies of any
part of the work should be mailed to:
Permissions, Harcourt Brace Jovanovich, Publishers,
Orlando, Florida 32887.

Library of Congress Cataloging-in-Publication Data
Ginsburg, Mirra.
The Chinese mirror.
"Gulliver books."
Summary: A retelling of a traditional Korean tale
in which a mirror brought from China causes confusion
within a family as each member looks in it and sees a
different stranger.
[1. Folklore—Korea] I. Zemach, Margot, ill.
II. Title.
PZ8.1.G455Ch 1987 398.2'Z 09519 [E] 86-22940
ISBN 0-15-200420-3

Printed in the United States of America
First edition
A B C D E

TO GRETA, MAYA, AND MARK

— M.G.

FOR ODETTE

— M.Z.

There was a time, long, long ago, when no one in our village had ever seen a mirror. One day a villager went on a distant journey, all the way to China.

There, he went into a store and saw a strange round
shiny thing. He looked at it, and a man's face looked back
at him. He smiled, and the man smiled back at him.
He stuck out his tongue, and the man stuck out
his tongue. "Sell it to me," he said to the storekeeper.
And he brought the mirror home with him.

At home he hid the mirror in a trunk, afraid its magic might be lost if everybody saw it. Once in a while he'd take it out secretly, laugh with pleasure, and then hide it again.

"Why is he laughing when there is nothing to laugh at?" his wife wondered, and began to watch him. One morning she saw him take a small round shiny thing out of the trunk, look into it, and smile. When he went out, she took the mirror and glanced into it.

"Oh, oh!" she cried.
"The cruel, faithless man!"
And she ran to her
mother-in-law, wailing,
"My faithless husband,
your son, brought home
a pretty, young wife from
China, and keeps her
hidden in the trunk. Look
at her, there she is!"

"Stop wailing," said
her mother-in-law, "and
let me see the young
beauty."

She glanced into the mirror, and burst out laughing. "My son may not be very clever," she said. "But why would he bring home a wrinkled old crone? No, there must be something else to it. He'd never get himself such a wife, it's just your foolish jealousy."

At that moment the man's father walked in

and wondered why his daughter-in-law was crying

and his wife laughing.

"Let me see for myself," he said.

He looked, and shrugged his shoulders, and said,
"You sillies. This is not a woman, either young or old.
It is our neighbor's grandpa, with his
bald head and gray beard."

They kept looking and looking. But the young wife
kept seeing a pretty young woman. The old woman
kept seeing a wrinkled old crone. The old man kept seeing
the neighbor's grandpa.

And none could convince the others that they were wrong.

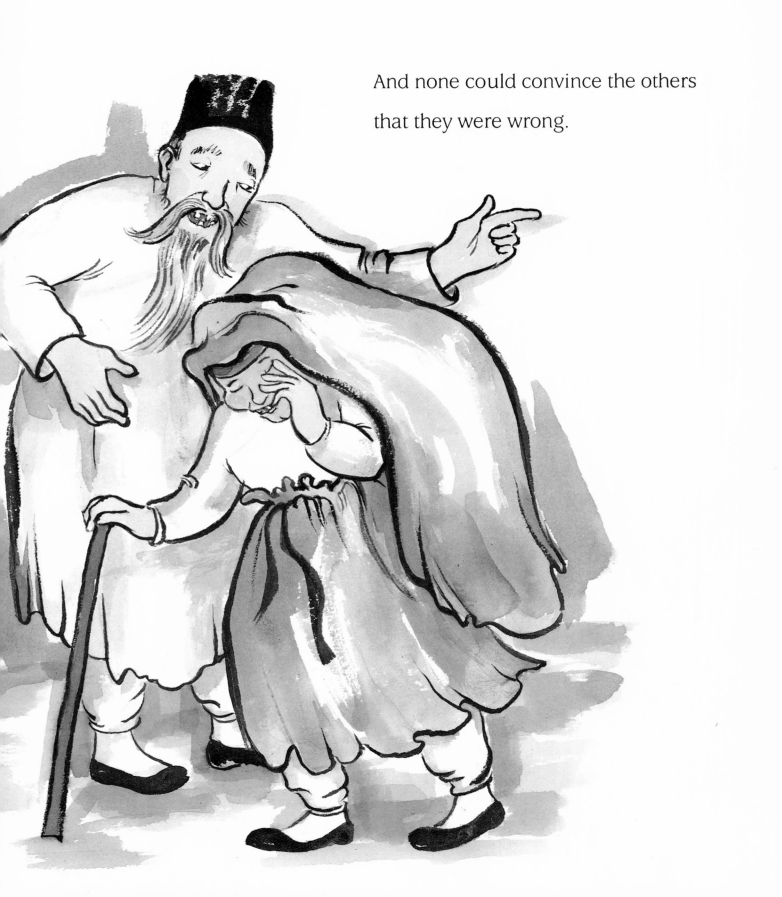

They put the mirror back in the trunk, still arguing.

Now, the man and his wife had a little son.

"What are they arguing about?"

he asked himself. "Let me see."

When they were all gone,
he took the mirror and
looked in, and saw a boy
with a nice round pebble
in his hand.

"Oh, oh!" he yelled.
"The nasty brat stole my
pebble!"

A neighbor happened to
be passing by.

"Why are you crying?" he asked.

"Who stole your pebble?"

The boy held out the mirror and the man looked into it.

"You big fat bully," he shouted.

"How dare you hurt little children?"

He banged his fist into the bully's face. Out flew the mirror, crashed against the wall, and scattered into a hundred shiny splinters.

And that was the end of the stranger who
looked at the traveler, the young beauty from China,
the wrinkled old crone, the neighbor's grandpa,
the nasty brat who stole pebbles, and the
big fat bully who hurt little boys.

The illustrations in this book were inspired
by the paintings of two eighteenth-century
Korean genre painters,
Sin Yun-bok and Kim Hong-do.

The illustrations in this book were done in watercolor on Crescent illustration board.
The text type was set in ITC Usherwood Book.
The display type was set via photo typositor in Auriol Bold.
Composed by Thompson Type, San Diego, California
Color separations were made by Heinz Weber Inc., Los Angeles, California.
Printed and bound by Horowitz/Rae Book Manufacturers, Fairfield, New Jersey
Production supervision by Warren Wallerstein and Ginger Boyer
Designed by Joy Chu